takes was run on June 19, 1867, at Jerome Park Race Course. The mile and five-eighths race was won by Ruthless in

873, and the Kentucky Derby from 1875. Triple Crown winners are: Sir Barton, 1919; Gallant Fox, 1930; Omaha, 1935; War

ffirmed, 1978. Seattle Slew, the longest-living Triple Crown winner, died May 7, 2002, of natural causes. He was 28. In

Secretariat's time, according to the Daily Racing Form, was 1:53⅖. That time has been equaled by Tank's Prospect, in 1985,

Gallant Man, which was 2:26⅗. Secretariat won the mile and a half Belmont by an astounding thirty-one lengths

ord "furlang," meaning the length of a furrow. Early Virginia tracks followed the oval furrows of tobacco farmers. The Darley

mported to Virginia in 1730. Secretariat descends from the Darley. Trainer Hollie Hughes called Secretariat "The Horse of the Century."

I RODE THE RED HORSE

DISCARD

the one horse in the heart
that runs
and runs

—"Horses," by Robert Dana

Library of Congress Control Number: 2002114041

ISBN 1-58150-096-3

Printed in Hong Kong
First Edition: April 2003

Distributed to the trade by
National Book Network
4720-A Boston Way, Lanham, MD 20706
1.800.462.6420

A Division of The Blood-Horse, Inc.
PUBLISHERS SINCE 1916
ECLIPSE PRESS

I RODE THE RED HORSE

SECRETARIAT'S BELMONT RACE

WRITTEN AND ILLUSTRATED BY

BARBARA M. LIBBY
IV

JE

The author wishes to credit the following:

Big Red of Meadow Stable: Secretariat, The Making of a Champion,
   by William Nack (A. Fields Books, © 1975, distributed by E. P. Dutton).
Secretariat, by Raymond G. Woolfe, Jr., © 1974 and 1981
   by Raymond G. Woolfe Jr.

I would like to thank the following people for their assistance
   in the creation of this book:

Ron Turcotte, who generously shared memories and information
William Nack
Norm Ward and **Walter Hillenmeyer** of Wood Lynn Farm
Pam Schapiro
John Englehardt and **Jo-Lynn Johnston** of River Downs Race Track
Anne Eberhardt and **Judy Grunwald** of The Blood-Horse, Inc.
Cathy Schenck, Librarian at Keeneland Association
Jacqueline Duke, editor
Brian Turner, book designer
Mark Stefan, for friendship as well as equine information
Sue Ellen Brown, Connie Trounstine, Leezie Borden, and **Maggie Leon,**
   for unflagging encouragement and humor.

My final thanks are to Mort for suggesting that I write about
   his favorite athlete, a horse.

to my parents

The papers called him Superhorse,

the Red Horse, and the Big Red Machine.

"Like a Train," one headline ran.

Eddie Sweat, his groom, called him Red, and later, Big Red.

I called him Red, or Big Boy, or Handsome.

Handsome? He was a burnished statue come to life,

glinting like a new copper penny,

the muscles and sinews and energy

almost more than the skin could hold.

Every switch of his tail had a flourish, like a movie star.

Photographers loved him.

And with all those good looks, he was a kind horse,

full of play and spirit. He'd grab the curry comb

right out of Sweat's hand, then drop it in the straw,

watching him with that eye. It was as though God decided

to create the perfect horse —

God and luck and centuries of breeding the best with the best,

from the Darley Arabian in 1700 to the powerful Bold Ruler, his sire.

His dam was Somethingroyal, by Princequillo.

The Princequillos could run all day,

so in the Sport of Kings

he was truly born a prince,

this big red horse with three white stockings

and a star on his forehead.

Riding him was the quiet in the eye

of a hurricane, all around us the heat

and grit and noise and effort.

There'd be that rhythmic bellows

of his lungs working.

He had a powerful push with his hind legs.

His forelegs snapped out for a stride of twenty-five feet.

Go easy, big boy, I'd whisper, and hold him back,

or, *Now big boy,* and give him his head.

The Belmont — what a day that was!

By afternoon the track was all

hot steam and dust, ninety degrees.

I was thinking about what Hollie Hughes

had told me. He was the senior horse trainer in America then.

He'd seen the first Big Red, Man o' War, run.

"Son," he said, "there is

no way you can get this horse beat today.

Just don't fall off. Believe me boy, you are riding

the greatest horse of all time and I have seen them all."

We moved into the gate.

There was the dark bay, Sham,

sweat beading down his neck.

The gate clanged open and we were flying!

I held tight to his red mane.

He wasn't holding back, not this time.

Easy big boy, I whispered, *you don't have to go yet,*

but he was running his own race.

We swept the quarter

and then the half-mile,

and it was five-eighths in :58 1/5,

faster than the brilliant Man o' War

or Citation had run that track.

He picked up speed. It was all on his own;

I asked for nothing.

The others were ten lengths behind.

All but Laffit Pincay on Sham. They'd pressed us

from the start, keeping it a sprinter's pace.

Sham's trainer wanted this one badly.

They'd come so close in the Derby and the Preakness,

he seemed a real contender, but now

the bay was laboring, and at the seven-eighths pole

something broke in him. He faded back

as my horse rounded the mile in 1:34 1/5

with a seven-length lead.

The rest was like a dream of flying.

We covered the mile and a quarter in 1:59,

faster than his own Kentucky Derby record.

Where were the others, My Gallant, Twice a Prince, Pvt. Smiles?

I turned to look, thinking *Don't fall off*!

Around us was a roisterous river of people cheering, waving,

pouring from the stands to press the rail.

The track announcer exclaimed,

"He is going to be the Triple Crown Winner!"

I looked at the teletimer — the record was 2:26 3/5 —

and there it was, blinking 2:19, 2:20...

so for the last seventy-five yards in the mile and a half race,

I hand-rode my horse, urging *Now, big boy! Now!*

We flew under the wire thirty-one lengths ahead,

and time stopped at 2:24.

That was our moment,

that moment in time never surpassed

on a track,

and I take no credit for what that horse did,

though I've ridden many horses,

and many of them fine.

It was his race all the way.

He's been called "The Horse of the Century,"

the greatest horse to ever run a track,

and I'm known as the jockey

who rode Secretariat,

our triumph etched

in time, in heart.

AFTERWORD

Called "The Horse of the Century," Meadow Stable's Secretariat was voted Horse of the Year as both a two- and three-year-old. Born March 30, 1970, he won the Sanford, Hopeful, Belmont Futurity, Laurel Futurity, and Garden State Stakes at two; at three, in addition to the Triple Crown, he won the Gotham Stakes, Arlington Invitational Stakes, the Marlboro Cup, the Man o' War Stakes, and Canadian International. After his three-year-old season, he retired to stud at Claiborne Farm in Kentucky, where he attracted more than 10,000 visitors annually.

At the age of 19, Secretariat contracted laminitis, a painful disease of the foot. Secretariat was euthanized on October 2, 1989, to prevent further suffering. An autopsy performed at the University of Kentucky determined that his heart, though normal, was twice the average size, which undoubtedly contributed to his great ability.

Secretariat was buried in an oak casket at Claiborne Farm next to his sire, Bold Ruler. Statues of him stand at Belmont Park and the Kentucky Horse Park. His 1973 Kentucky Derby record has yet to be broken and his 1973 Belmont Stakes time is still the fastest in the world for a mile and a half on a dirt track.

Secretariat won the mile and a quarter Kentucky Derby in 1:59 2/5. He won the Belmont in 2:24 by a history-making thirty-one lengths.

Ron Turcotte was Canada's leading jockey in 1962 and 1963. He moved to the United States and became a leading jockey in Maryland and New York, riding champions like Tom Rolfe, Damascus, Shuvee, and Riva Ridge, the 1972 Kentucky Derby and Belmont Stakes winner. He was awarded the Order of Canada, the nation's highest honor for civilians, by England's Queen Elizabeth in 1974.

In 1978, five years after riding Secretariat to the Triple Crown, Ron went down with a horse during a race at Belmont Park. He suffered a spinal injury, which paralyzed him from the chest down. Facing his disability with great courage, Ron and his wife Gaetane moved their family back home to New Brunswick, Canada, in 1979.

Ron was elected to the Racing Hall of Fame in 1979 and has received several awards for his humanitarian work in Canada and the United States. He continues to receive requests for autographs and pictures. Ron supports numerous worthy causes, including those for the disabled, and participates in an active, outdoor life.

The phrase "Triple Crown" was first used by writer Bryan Field in the New York Times *in 1930. The first Belmont*

3:05. Belmont Park opened in 1905. White carnations are the official flowers of the Belmont Stakes. The Preakness dates from

Admiral, 1937; Whirlaway, 1941; Count Fleet, 1943; Assault, 1946; Citation, 1948; Secretariat, 1973; Seattle Slew, 1977;

the Kentucky Derby, which he won in 1:59⅖, Secretariat broke Northern Dancer's 1964 record of 2:00. In the Preakness,

and Louis Quatorze, in 1996. In the 1973 Belmont Stakes, Secretariat broke the 1957 track and stakes record of

in 2:24, still the fastest time on the dirt at that distance. The word "furlong," one-eighth of a mile, comes from the Old Englis

Arabian was bought by Thomas Darley in Aleppo, Syria, in 1704, then sent to Yorkshire, England. Bulle Rock, his son, was